HERNANDO FANDANGO
The Great Dancing Dog!
By Rachel Swirles

For Lizzie, who's
been with me all
the way x   R.S.

This edition published by Parragon in 2013
Parragon
Chartist House
15-17 Trim Street
Bath BA1 1HA, UK
www.parragon.com

Published by arrangement with Meadowside Children's Books
185 Fleet Street, London, EC4A 2HS

Text and Illustrations © Rachel Swirles

ISBN 978-1-4723-1854-1
Printed in China

Bath • New York • Singapore • Hong Kong • Cologne • Delhi
Melbourne • Amsterdam • Johannesburg • Shenzhen

He's clever, adventurous, courageous, and mighty,
(And ever so handy for storing a nightie),

HERNANDO FANDANGO, pajama-case dog,
Is the very best friend of Miss Adelaide Mogg.

Now, of all the fun things they did together,
Dancing gave them the greatest pleasure!

In Adelaide's room they would
practice each day ...

JAZZ,

Ballroom
dancing,

Tap,

and

Ballet!

Secretly dreaming of a shiny dance floor,
With a crowd of fans cheering

"ENCORE!
ENCORE!"

And, as it happened, by
the most amazing
of chances ...

Adelaide's parents were REAL ballroom dancers!

The foxtrot, the rumba,
   the American smooth,
The quick step, the samba—
   they knew every move!

Hernando and Adelaide never grew tired,
Of watching them dance, they felt so inspired!

Now Adelaide's parents were preparing to be
Part of a dance show, to compete on TV!

The big day was near,

so they shimmied

and hopped,

They twirled and whirled,

and danced ...

till they dropped!

The competition day duly arrived,
The dancing began, they waltzed, then they jived.

The Moggs looked so graceful, they'd practiced so much,
Surely nothing could come between them and the cup!
But ...

With the cameras rolling
and MILLIONS tuned in,
To see all the couples
doing their thing ...

Two couples collided ...

a dancer's **worst** fear,

A pair of **sprained** ankles—the Moggs couldn't appear!

The host shouted out,

"Do we have
any dancers?"

Adelaide knew this was
the rarest of chances.

She longed to cry out,
But she wasn't that brave,

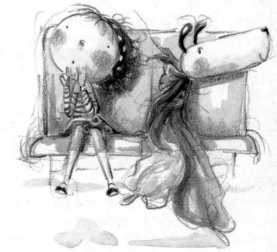

And already a figure
had taken the stage!

Can you guess who it was,
who could waltz, jive, and tango ...?

Of course—it was ...

HERNANDO FANDANGO!

Courageous and mighty,

pajama-case dog,

Reached for the hand

of Miss Adelaide Mogg.

She smiled at Hernando
and, taking his paw,
Took a deep breath
and stepped onto the floor!

So, they started to waltz, Miss Mogg and her hound,
And, as they danced, the best friends found
That their dream had come true!
They swished round the floor,

The music was playing!
The crowd gave a ROAR!

Their waltz
was **divine,**

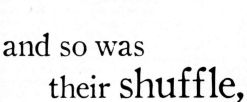

and so was
their **shuffle,**

Their **cha-cha-cha**
caused quite a **kerfuffle!**

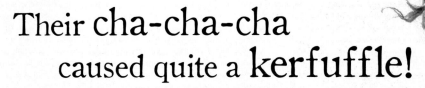

And, lo and behold,
for the next **big band** number,
Hernando and Adelaide
were **dancing** the **rumba!**

Now for the voting, from across the nation!
Who would be the new **dance sensation?**

(Long pause
for effect …)

"Ladies and gentlemen,
the winners are …"

"Adelaide Mogg
and
HERNANDO FANDANGO,
the Great Dancing Dog!"

Everyone cheered, the nation was right,
Hernando and Adelaide were the stars of the night.

So Adelaide and Hernando held hands—and paws—
And they took their bow to rapturous applause.

He's clever, adventurous, courageous, and mighty,
(And ever so handy for storing a nightie),

Hernando Fandango, pajama-case dog,
Is the very best friend of Miss Adelaide Mogg.